SPRING HARE

Eugene Yelchin

Henry Holt and Company

NEW YORK

To Mary

Henry Holt and Company

Publishers since 1866

175 Fifth Avenue, New York, New York 10010

mackids.com

Henry Holt® is a registered trademark of Macmillan Publishing Group, LLC.

ISBN 978-1-62779-392-6

LCCN 2016932984

Our books may be purchased in bulk for promotional, educational, or business use.
Please contact your local bookseller or the Macmillan Corporate and Premium Sales Department at
(800) 221-7945 ext. 5442 or by e-mail at MacmillanSpecialMarkets@macmillan.com.

First Edition—2017 / Designed by April Ward
The artist used gouache, acrylic, oil pastels, and colored pencils on cut paper to create the illustrations for this book.
Printed in China by RR Donnelley Asia Printing Solutions Ltd., Dongguan City, Guangdong Province

1 3 5 7 9 10 8 6 4 2

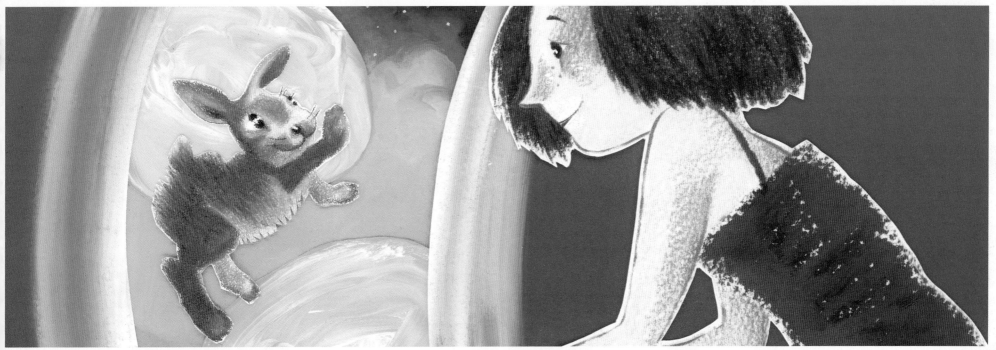